Harry the Poisonous Centipede

A story to make you squirm

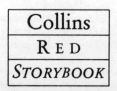

Collins
RED
STORYBOOK

Also by Lynne Reid Banks

The Adventures of King Midas
The Magic Hare
The Indian in the Cupboard
Return of the Indian
The Secret of the Indian
The Mystery of the Cupboard
The Key to the Indian
The Farthest Away Mountain
I, Houdini
The Fairy Rebel
Angela and Diabola

First published in Great Britain by CollinsChildren'sBooks in 1996

CollinsChildren'sBooks is a division of HarperCollins*Publishers* Ltd,
77-85 Fulham Palace Road, Hammersmith, London W6 8JB

The HarperCollins website address is
www.**fire**and**water**.com

15 17 16

ISBN 0 00 675197-0

**Printed and bound in Great Britain by
Omnia Books Ltd, Glasgow**

Harry the Poisonous Centipede

A story to make you squirm

LYNNE REID BANKS

Illustrated by Tony Ross

CollinsChildren'sBooks
An imprint of HarperCollins Publishers

For Emily

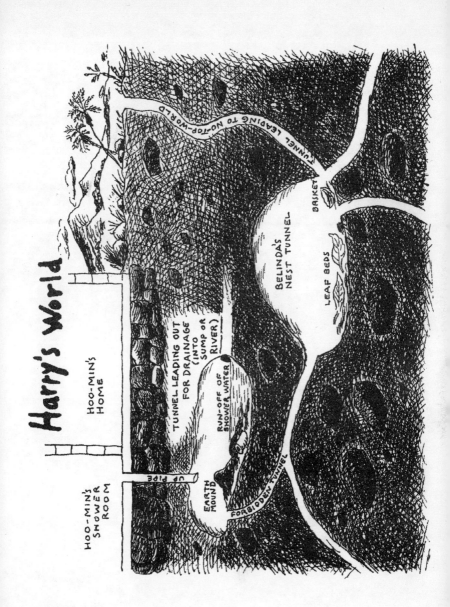

Harry's World

1. About Harry

Harry was a poisonous centipede.

You may think that's not a very nice thing to be. But Harry thought it was fine. He'd never been anything else, and he liked being what he was.

If you'd told him centipedes are nasty scary creepy-crawlies, he would have been very surprised and rather hurt.

And if you'd told him that biting things with poisonous pincers was wrong or cruel, he would probably have told you not to be ridiculous. How else would he get anything to eat, or defend himself from creatures wanting to eat *him*?

Of course, you couldn't have talked to Harry like that, even if you'd met him, because he couldn't have understood you. Harry could only speak to other centipedes, in Centipedish. In fact, his real name wasn't Harry at all. It was (as nearly as I can write it) Hxzltl.

Hxzltl?

Yes. You can see the problem at once. There are no vowel-sounds in Centipedish, just a sort of very faint crackling. What you could do is put in some vowel-sounds – some a's, e's, i's, o's and u's – so that you can try to say his real name. Then you could call him Hixzalittle. Or Hoxzalottle. Or perhaps even Haxzaluttle. But still you wouldn't be anywhere near the real sound of his name.

Which is why I call him Harry.

He lived in a very hot country – what we call the Tropics – with his mother.

Now, please don't start asking what *her* name was. Oh no. Please. Oh... All right. Here goes. It was Bkvlbbchk. Bikvilababchuk? Bokvaliboobchak? Bakvolobibchawk? I don't know. Why bother? We'll never get it right. Let's call her Belinda.

Belinda was also, of course, a poisonous centipede. A very large one – a good eight inches long, or twenty centimetres, if you want to be metric about it. Just imagine, eight inches of shiny, black, swift-moving centipede – a twenty-centi-centipede! Her body was something like a caterpillar's, in segments,

but covered with hard, shiny, dark stuff –
a sort of suit of armour, which is called a
cuticle.

Now, if you know a bit of Latin you'll
know that "centipede" means "one
hundred feet". Some kinds of centipede
do have that many, but Harry's kind
didn't. Harry and his mother had twenty-
one segments with one pair of legs to
each segment. Which makes forty-two
legs. Each.

Quite a lot to keep track of, when
you think about it, but neither Belinda
nor Harry ever did think about it. Any
more than you think how difficult –
Harry would have said, impossible – it
is to move about on two legs. They just
did it.

And did it, when they had to, very, very fast indeed.

Harry actually didn't know just how fast he could run, until the Dreadful Time when, despite his mother's sternest warning, he went Up the Up-Pipe. Which is the story I'm going to tell you.

When I get round to it. There are some other stories to tell first.

2. Belinda Tells a Scary Story

Harry, as I told you, lived in a hot country. But he didn't know that for a long time, because he didn't live on the surface of the earth where the sun shone a lot. He lived in a mass of dark, cool tunnels under the ground.

He slept all through the day. But at night he would wake up and run along these lovely earthy tunnels, looking for things to eat. What things? Well, if you must know:

worms,

slugs,

beetles,  spiders.

All kinds of insects and creepy-crawlies that were smaller than him.

He would chase after them, bite them, and, when the poison from his poison-claws had paralysed them, crunch them up. Well, crunch if they were crunchy, like beetles, or munch if they were munchy, like worms.

Belinda, being much more than twice his size, could tackle big things like toads, small snakes, young mice and lizards. But then, she could go up to the surface to hunt. Only for a short time, though. Centipedes mustn't get too dry or they can't breathe, and it's much easier to keep damp underground.

If she heard something thumping about on the surface that sounded good to eat, she'd nip along an up-going tunnel, scurry to the thumping thing, whatever it was, and if it wasn't *too* big she would bite it with her poisonous pincers and drag it back down the tunnel to share it with Harry.

Belinda was a very good mother.

When Harry and her other babies first came out of their eggs, she'd made something like a little basket to keep them in, and tended them carefully until they were old enough to fend for themselves.

All her other many children had gone off and left her, as young centipedes usually do, but Harry stayed. He loved her and she loved him, calling him love-names like "best-in-my-nest" and "pride-of-my-basket". She was always scared that something might happen to him, so she carefully warned him of dangers.

Of course he didn't take much notice. He was a big, strong, armoured centi (that's a child centipede) with two fine poison-claws, who could run faster than anything he'd ever met. What could hurt him?

"Lots of things," Belinda said firmly. "There are many things bigger than you, Hxzltl. When you're grown up and go up to the big, open, no-top-world – and you *must not do so before* – you'll find you're not the biggest thing around, by any means – or even the fastest!"

And she told him about flying things that swooped down and grabbed you, and great legless belly-crawlers, bigger than the tunnels the centipedes lived in, and enormous hairy things with huge sharp teeth and hot breath that could run even faster than the fastest centipede.

But the most awful things of all, Belinda told him – the biggest and the most terrifyingly dangerous – were Hoo-Mins. (Of course she pronounced it H-Mns.)

"I've nearly been killed by a Hoo-Min," his mother told him in a hushed tone. "Twice."

"Mama!"

"Oh yes! Once when I couldn't find food in the tunnels, I had to go up in the bright-time. All that bright light muddled me, and I got too far from the tunnel entrance. I was running back to it when a black shadow fell on me. Well, you don't know about shadows because you've never been out when big-yellow-ball is shining, but it's a dark thing that falls on you. And when you feel that shadow, you have to run like *mad*!"

"Why, is it heavy?"

"No. It doesn't weigh anything, itself. But behind it there is always *something*. And this *something*, this time, was a huge heavy thing that came crashing down. It just missed me! I *just* ran out in time! And although I ran as fast as I could run, this huge heavy thing kept up with me, and came crashing down again and again!"

Harry shuddered. "What happened, Mama?"

"I dodged!

I zigzagged!

17

I ran as never before! Suddenly I saw a tree with some leaves lying under it, and I raced for it, and dived under the nearest leaf. But I didn't stop there. And just as well!

"As I ran under the leaves, hunting for a hole, the crashing thing came down just in front of me! I had to turn and run back into the open. Then I ran in every direction.

"Thank goodness I found a hole and rushed down it just as the Thing came smashing down again. Oh Hxzltl, you can't think how nearly you lost your mama that time!"

"And that was a Hoo-Min that was chasing you? How do you know?"

"Because, when I got my breath back and got nice and damp again – as well as nearly getting squashed, I'd nearly Dried Out! – I peeped out of the hole, and saw it, walking away. I realised then that the crashing thing was its foot. It only had two, but they were ENORMOUS, Hxzltl!"

"How big, Mama?"

"As long as me and then as long as me again! And that's just its foot!" She stood in front of him, waving her feelers in a very solemn way. "And now that you are a big centi, I have something very important and dangerous to show you."

3. The Warning

She led him through their usual tunnels, and then turned off, along one she had often told him never to go down. It sloped downward, deep into the earth, and they followed it until they found themselves in a big kind of cave.

It felt very damp here – extra damp. There was a gleam down below – a pool! Harry got excited.

"Oooh, Mama! Look at that water! Is it like the sea? Can I play Sea-Centipedes?"

Harry had heard many stories about his cousins, who long ago had moved from earth-tunnels to homes by the ocean.

But Belinda shook her head. "No, Hxzltl! This is no place to play! It's very, very dangerous. Now, come over here, and look up."

Harry could now see that there was a faint light in the cave. It was coming from a tunnel above their heads that seemed to go straight up.

"What a funny tunnel!" he said. "It's so straight! And its walls are as shiny as your cuticle, Mama!"

"Yes. No centipede burrowed this one! You can see it's not made of earth like our regular tunnels. It's made of some hard shiny stuff. It's not easy to get a grip on with your feet. But just the same it's possible to climb it. I know, because—" She stopped suddenly. "Only you mustn't, Hxzltl. Do you hear me? *You must not go Up the Up-Pipe.*"

"Why not?"

"Because it leads into the Place of Hoo-Mins," she said in that same hushed voice she had used before, the one that made Harry's cuticle go cold.

"How do you know, Mama?"

"I would rather not say."

"Have *you* been Up the Up-Pipe? Was that the second time you just escaped from a Hoo-Min?"

Belinda turned her head away. A long shudder ran along her back.

"Yes. When I was young and knew nothing of danger. I had no mama to guide me. But you have, pride-of-my-basket. So listen: Never, ever, ever, go Up the Up-Pipe. Because if you do, you may never come down again."

4. The Pool

Harry wasn't stupid. His mother had really frightened him about the Hoo-Mins. He didn't even want to explore the Up-Pipe.

But the pool underneath it was something else.

Every young centipede learns about its cousins the marine centipedes, and young ones always play at being able to swim in the sea, and hide in the rocky crevices between the high and low tidelines, and live in empty barnacle shells or sea-worm tubes.

Harry couldn't swim. But he loved

water. There wasn't much rain in the country where he lived, but just occasionally there would be a storm, and rainwater would flow into the tunnels and make puddles. They weren't very deep and the water soon seeped away, but while they lasted, Harry would paddle in them and pretend to be a marine centipede.

He was pretty sure he would be able to swim if he ever found a puddle deep enough to try.

And now he knew about the pool under the Up-Pipe, he kept thinking about it. He could pretend it was the sea and that he was a fearless marine centipede. Why shouldn't he learn to swim, if they could? It would be such fun to take his mother to the pool one day, and pretend to fall in to give her a fright, and then show her how he could swim.

So one day, or rather one night, he

scurried off down the forbidden tunnel that led to the pool and the Up-Pipe.

He ran down the earthy slope to the edge of the water.

It was dark and scummy – not nice clean water like the rain made. It didn't smell nice, either. (This was because the Up-Pipe was a drain, which carried away a Hoo-Min's dirty shower-water. But Harry didn't know that.)

He was determined not to be put off. He turned round and tried the water with his back feelers.

That was all right. So he walked backwards until his rear five segments were in the pool. Six. Seven. Eight. Nine. Now he was nearly halfway in, and his tail-parts began to float to the top.

He couldn't hold them down. Was he swimming? He wriggled his rear nine pairs of legs and his body moved about. That was swimming, surely? He backed a little further. And a little further...

Whoops!

With only a third of his body-length still on shore, he began to lose his grip on the earth with his front legs.

He clawed frantically with his first seven pairs of legs, digging the tiny claws on their tips into the soft, wet earth. But there was too much of him already floating in the scummy water. Something seemed to be pulling at him, dragging him away from the safe ground.

But Belinda was far away and couldn't catch his signals.

Harry clutched and tugged, and sent out signals of distress, but nobody came, and the water kept pulling until first one, then another, and finally all seven front segments left the shore. Harry found himself struggling in the deep, dark, bad-smelling water!

Kicking and squirming, he was carried along through the darkness. He kept going under, and the water entered his breathing holes (he had one in each segment). He would blow it out and pop to the surface again but he knew he couldn't go on doing this for long. He was choking – choking all along his length. It was terrible! He was going to drown!

He sank beneath the surface once again. "I'm dead!" was his last conscious thought. "Oh, Mama!"

5. Harry Upside Down

He woke slowly. He felt awful. Truly awful.

The world was all wrong, somehow.

Harry's eyes weren't good anyway and now they were useless. They seemed to be staring straight into the earth. Something hard was pressing on the back of his head. His legs weren't touching anything. He kicked them about, trying to run, but it was no use. He thrust out his poison-claws, which was always his reaction to danger. They closed on emptiness.

WHERE was he?

How was he?

He slowly realised how he was. He was upside down, a position he'd never been in before. That was why he felt so funny.

He didn't realise how lucky he'd been. He'd been washed to the side of the pool, or stream, or whatever it was, on to his back. Because of this, all the water that had got into his breathing holes had drained out. Of course he still couldn't breathe very well because some of the holes were now blocked by the ground.

He struggled to right himself, rocking

this way and that, wriggling and twisting. With a final jerk, he managed to get his front half round the right way. After that, it wasn't hard to turn the rest of himself.

He looked around. The pool wasn't there any more. Just a long muddy channel. It seemed that the water flowed down it, like the rainwater in Harry's regular tunnels, and then soaked away somehow.

Harry tested his twenty-one segments by lifting them one by one off the ground, and all his forty-two feet by moving them in the air, in a sort of ripple, first along one side of him, then along the other. They seemed to work. What a relief!

He tried to run. He found he could!

He did. He ran as fast as he could run in the direction of home. (He knew by instinct which direction to run in.)

As he ran, he tried to think. Should he tell his mother what had happened to him?

Probably better not. Even though he hadn't done the one thing she'd told him never to do – go Up the Up-Pipe into the Place of Hoo-Mins.

6. The Lie

"Hxzltl! Where HAVE you been? I've been really worried about you!"

"Oh... I've just been – er – you know—"

"Hunting?"

"Er – yes."

"Any luck?"

Now she mentioned it, Harry realised that he hadn't eaten since those twenty-five ants' eggs he'd had for breakfast and that he was absolutely starving. He shook his head.

Belinda gave a centipedic smile (which she did by waving her front feelers in a particular way). "I'm glad, because look what I've brought you! Your favourite!"

And she stepped aside and showed him a large, crunchy, juicy treat – his favourite indeed! It was a locust, which is like a very big grasshopper.

"Mama! Wow! Thanks! Can I eat it now?"

"Of course you can, best-in-my-nest!" she said proudly.

He ate the locust greedily, head first, although the head was the best bit and he usually saved it till last. By the time he'd crunched the last leg, he realised he wasn't feeling very happy.

You can guess why, of course. He felt bad because he'd lied to his mother. But he didn't see how he could have told her he'd been so stupid and nearly got drowned.

Still. It wasn't as if she'd absolutely forbidden him to play near the water. She'd only forbidden him to go Up the Up-Pipe, to the Place of Hoo-Mins. And he hadn't done *that*.

He wasn't going to do it, either. Not him. No, never. He didn't want to mess with those awful Hoo-Mins.

And he probably wouldn't have done, if it hadn't been for Grnddjl.

Don't even try it. Let's call him George.

7. About George

George was Harry's best friend. They'd been best friends almost from the time they'd come out of their mothers' baskets.

George didn't live with his mother. He'd run off and left her, as most centis do, as soon as he could run, and he called Harry a sissyfeelers for wanting to stick with his mother.

George lived and hunted alone, and because he was still very young and couldn't always catch anything, he often felt hungry.

Then he saw the sense of having a mother.

He would come creeping along to Belinda's nest-tunnel and lie there, waving his front feelers feebly, looking really pathetic, until she would say, "Oh, all right then, George, you'd better come and have a bite of lizard with us. But stop teasing Harry for still living with his mama!"

Belinda worried a lot about Harry being such good friends with George. Harry got himself into enough scrapes without George leading him into all sorts of adventures.

"You don't have to do everything Grnddjl does, you know," she would often tell Harry. "He's a very foolish and naughty centi."

"Don't worry, Mama. I can think for myself," Harry would say.

But it's very difficult, when your friend wants to do something that sounds exciting, to be a "dry sandbed" (which is like a wet blanket with us) and say you don't want to join in because your mama wouldn't like it.

So when one day George suggested that it was time they climbed out on to the no-top-world to do a bit of real hunting, Harry only hung back a little. He was really very keen himself to go out and see the surface world outside.

"Only we'll have to watch out for flying swoopers, and belly wrigglers, and furry biters, and especially Hoo-Mins," he said.

George looked taken aback, but only for a moment.

"Oh, I know all about those things," he said in a pooh-poohing way. "They're so big I don't know how you can help smelling them coming, or feeling the vibrations. And we won't go far from a hole. Well, come on then! Are you a scaredy-ant, or what?"

8. The Thing

Harry said no more and followed him along a tunnel that led to the no-top-world.

It was night. The two young centis poked their feelers out, side by side, and felt around, and sniffed the outside air. It smelt wildly exciting. They couldn't see much with their weak little eye-clusters, but their feelers told them there were lots of interesting things about.

"I smell food!" whispered George.

"Me, too! What is it?" Harry whispered back.

George crawled a little further out of

the hole, and waved his feelers some more.

"It's something lovely and meaty, anyway! Let's follow its smell and find out what it is!"

They crawled swiftly out and ran along the ground. It was great to be outdoors! Harry wondered why his mother had never brought him before. He could feel the fresh air along his segments, and knew by instinct that he mustn't stay out long – that air could make him Dry Out. Meanwhile, this was the best fun he'd ever had!

George stopped so suddenly that Harry ran over the top of him.

"Smell that!" George crackled quietly.

The most wonderful, warm, juicy, meaty smell came to Harry's feelers. It was very close!

"What is it? A mouse?"

"No. I don't know what it is. It's over there! Let's go and get it!"

"It might be too big..."

"It's not. Can't you feel the vibrations from its feet? It's not much bigger than us! Come on, let's go for it! Get your poison-pincers ready!"

George started to run, and Harry, who was still on his back, fell off. He righted himself and ran after George. He didn't want to be left behind!

They turned a corner beside a large stone. And suddenly, they saw it!

In fact they practically ran right into it.

It was the fearsomest looking creature they had ever seen. It was a thing called a

mole-cricket: like an enormous furry cockroach armed with a pair of huge front paws like a bear's.

George reared up in terror, and his top half did a swift U-turn in the air. "Let's get out of here!" he crackled shrilly, and turned to flee.

As George spun round, The Thing turned as well, and came lumbering after him.

George was well on his way, but Harry wasn't. He was so frightened he just stood there, and The Thing came running towards him, looking like a charging rhinoceros would to us.

At the last second, Harry tried to dodge out of its path, but The Thing turned its great ugly head, and its terrible claw-paws made a swipe at Harry.

Harry instinctively whisked his tail and gave The Thing a clout. That made it jump, just long enough for Harry to stick his head under it and get in a good poisonous bite on its belly.

It went stiff. Its claw-paws drooped to the ground. In another second, its thick jointed legs had collapsed under it, and it fell with a thud.

Right on top of Harry!

9. George to the Rescue

Harry's legs collapsed too. All forty-two of them.

His head and his first four segments were pinned under the paralysed mole-cricket. He was stunned. He lay still for a minute and then began wriggling and writhing. He tried to pull backwards. He tried to lift his head and shift the weight off him.

He couldn't. The Thing was too heavy.

He tried to call George. He couldn't. But he did the next best thing.

He lifted his back five segments clear

off the ground and waved a desperate
signal with his tail feelers.

George, who was practically back at
the hole, had felt the vibration as The
Thing fell. Now he looked back. He
caught the signal Harry was sending with
his tail feelers.

He hesitated.

The signal Harry was sending said,
"Help! Help! Help!" But the signal
George was getting was more like,
"Danger! Danger! Danger!"

He wanted to keep on running, back

down the hole, to safety.

But Harry was his best friend. He couldn't just leave him to the monster.

He turned and raced back as fast as he could. Which was very fast.

As soon as he saw what had happened, he crackled loudly: "Hang on, Hx! I'm here! I'll soon have you out!"

Then he caught hold of one of the mole-cricket's legs in his mouth, and pulled. He twisted and turned and jerked his head. The mole-cricket was a dead weight. It was much heavier than anything George had ever tried to drag before.

But at last it started to shift.

As soon as Harry felt it begin to move, he made a strong effort himself, and soon got his head and front segments free.

"Thanks, Grndd! Phew! If you hadn't come back, I'd have just stayed there till I starved, or something Got me!"

10. The Feast

George rubbed his round, hard head-segment against Harry's. "You were braver than me! You bit it! It's ours now. What shall we do?"

"Drag it home and eat it for dinner!"

"YES!"

They started to drag and pull it with all their might.

Between them they got it back to the hole and then went behind it and tipped it down. It started to slide down the tunnel. They ran after it and pushed and shoved some more.

It slid right to the bottom. After that, they crawled over it and dragged it along to Belinda's nest-tunnel.

They arrived at last. They were tired out. Belinda was there. She didn't say anything at first, just raised herself up and felt the mole-cricket all over with her front feelers.

Then she dropped down on to all forty-two legs again. She turned right round in a tight circle several times, which is what she always did when she just didn't know what to say or do.

"Oh, you bad, brave, naughty, wonderful centis!" she said at last. "You've been up to the no-top-world, haven't you? What am I to do with you?"

"Could you just help us take The Thing's fur off so we can all eat it for dinner?" asked Harry in a small, but proud, crackle.

His mother wrapped her first seven

pairs of legs round him and gave him a terrific hug.

Then she hugged George too.

They had a feast. Belinda had never tasted mole-cricket before. She knew what they were, all right, and told the centis that they burrowed under the ground – making useful tunnels – and ate roots, mainly, but that they were so frightening-looking that she had never dared try to attack one.

She said, though, that the two centis had been very foolish to go to the no-top-world without her and that they weren't to do it again until they were grown up. "Now, promise me."

Harry was just going to promise, when George said, "Hey! What was that vibration? Was it a toad, or just a grasshopper?"

Belinda rushed up the nearest tunnel to see what it was, and forgot to make them promise.

If centipedes could wink, George would have winked at Harry.

11. George Wants a Thrill

After their adventure with the mole-cricket, George wanted to do something even more exciting.

Ordinary mischief was no good any more. He wanted another big thrill.

Even if he had promised Harry's mother not to go back to the surface, I'm afraid he might not have kept it. But anyway, he hadn't. So he started to make regular trips.

Harry didn't go with him.

"What's the matter, sissyfeelers, scaredy-ant, why won't you come?" taunted George, who didn't like having adventures by himself.

"I don't want to worry Mama," muttered Harry uncomfortably.

George gave a great crackle and waved his front feelers crazily in all directions. (That is a centi's way of laughing mockingly.)

"Mama's centi! Mama's centi!" he teased.

"Anyway, it's silly," said Harry, when

he could make himself heard. "We don't want to get hurt or killed."

"Last night I was chased by a hairy biter," boasted George. "It jumped down out of a tree and chased me. But I felt it hit the ground and I ran straight between its legs and up the tree and into a crack where it couldn't get me! I wasn't scared! Big clumsy thing, I heard it coming a mile off!"

Harry wasn't sure whether to believe him. George was a big show-off.

"Maybe you're braver than me," he said. "But I've got more sense than you, anyway!"

And he turned and ran down a tunnel.

After a bit, George came after him.

"All right. All right. If you don't want to go up to the no-top-world, think of something exciting to do down here."

Harry didn't say anything. Something

more than just exciting had popped into his head at once.

He moved his front feelers about in a thoughtful way. George guessed that he had something interesting in his mind.

"What? WHAT?" he crackled, waving his legs in ripples of excitement along his sides.

"The Up-Pipe. But we mustn't."

"What's the Up-Pipe?"

"It's a kind of tunnel. But we can't go up it."

"Mama said not to, I suppose!" jeered George.

"Yes, she did. Because it leads to the Place of Hoo-Mins."

George stopped making ripples. "Hoo-Mins? What's that?"

"I thought you said you knew about Hoo-Mins."

George looked uncomfortable.

"I thought they were just another kind

of hairy biter," he said. "Go on, then. Tell me what they are."

Harry told him, as well as he could. He'd never seen one himself.

"Well, you know we sometimes hear very big vibrations. And you know how Mama never, ever goes up to see what they are. That's them. They're giant two-legses. As big as trees. Each one of their feet is as big as a whole hairy biter. And they're fast. They try to Get you by smashing you with shadows." (Harry had got in a bit of a muddle.)

"Can you eat them?"

"*Eat them?* Oh, sure, of course! A nice little snack!" George looked blank. "Well, could you drag a tree home, stupid?"

They both started laughing. They laughed till they rolled on their backs. Then suddenly George jerked himself right side up and said, "I want to see one."

"They only come out in the bright-time," Harry said.

"We could stay awake and go up in the bright-time."

"Up the Up-Pipe?" asked Harry in a shocked crackle.

"Are they only up the Up-Pipe?"

"No. Mama told me one chased her on the no-top-world."

"So, we could just peep at them through a hole," said George. "But show me the Up-Pipe first."

"No."

"Oh, go on! It can't hurt to look! I dare you to show it to me."

Harry couldn't resist a dare. So he said, "All right, then. But remember. It's not the Up-Pipe that's dangerous. It's the Hoo-Mins who live at the top."

12. Looking at the Up-Pipe

Harry led George along the forbidden tunnel to the pool. As before, there was a faint light in the earth-cave. The two centis stood under the light and stared up.

"The Up-Pipe!" breathed George. He was impressed.

"Mama says the sides are slippery and hard to grip," said Harry.

"I bet I could climb it!" said George.

"How could we reach it?"

"Easy. We could pile up some earth. Then if you stood on the pile with most of your segments upright, I could climb up you and get hold with my front four or six feet. When I'd got a good grip, you could climb up the rest of my segments. I'd leave them hanging down for you."

"What would you hold on to?"

"See that rough place near the beginning of the pipe? I'd hold that. We could do it. I know we could. Oh, come on, Hx, let's!"

Harry shook his round little head.

"And what when we got to the top? What if a Hoo-Min saw us?"

"We'd turn right round and go back down! If they're as big as you said, they couldn't possibly follow us!"

And George at once started scuffling about with his front eight pairs of legs and his head, pushing loose earth into a pile like a platform, under the Up-Pipe.

Suddenly, far above their heads, they heard something.

It was a thumping. A noise of something heavy, coming down bump, right over where they were!

They both went tense. Harry said, "It's a Hoo-Min! Let's go!"

George said, "Wait."

They crouched there on the earth-pile. The thumping went on. It wasn't regular. There was a thump. A pause. Another thump.

Nothing else. happened. At first.

"It's walking! When it stops, we'll go up!" crackled George.

And he would have, too. Only suddenly there was another noise.

It was a swish. A pattering like rain on the surface. And then—!

A great gurgle!

A WOOSH!

And before they could think what to do, something came plummeting down towards them!

13. Harry Learns to Swim

What came down the Up-Pipe now was like a post that Harry had once seen, being driven down into the earth. Only this post wasn't made of wood.

It was made of water.

When it hit them it nearly knocked them out. They were washed off the mound of earth. The mound of earth was swept away. The water began to carry them along in a gurgling, bubbling torrent.

Harry recovered first. He managed to grab George with his poison-pincers as he was swept past. Of course he didn't inject

his poison. He just used the pincers to
hold on to his friend.

They clung together. The water-post
was still coming down, but they weren't
under it any more.

The water was all around them like a
living thing, but for Harry, this wasn't
new. He'd been through it before. He
knew what to do.

"Swim!" he crackled. "Ripple your
legs! Make for the earth!"

The water was rushing, pulling,
carrying them. George just threshed
around uselessly. But Harry swam! He
actually swam, just as if he'd been a
true marine centi! When he had to, he
found he could. If he hadn't, George
would have drowned.

He managed to signal to George to
keep upright so his breathing holes didn't
get swamped. He even managed to hold
George up till he got the idea. He

dragged him along, fighting the strong current.

And by swimming his hardest, Harry made it to the edge of the water.

They dragged themselves on to the black, muddy shore. They lay there, exhausted.

George couldn't make even a faint crackle. He just lay there.

Harry got up slowly and shook the water off his cuticle. He rubbed the water out of his eyes with his pincers. He pushed George.

"Come on! Get up! You're all right."

George lifted his head. Centipedes can't cry, but if they could, George would have been crying.

"No, I'm not. I'm not," he said, and dropped his head again. His feelers stretched miserably along the ground. "I think I'm dead."

"You are not. You're as alive as I am."

Harry gave him a non-poisonous pinch with his pincers.

"Ouch! Don't DO that!" George sat up and shook himself.

Harry was feeling very pleased with himself. He could really and truly swim! And he'd rescued George – saved his life!

"What about the Up-Pipe then?" he teased. "Shall we go?"

"Oh shut up," said George. But he got up and trailed after Harry along the edge of the rushing river of water, back to where they'd been.

The water wasn't rushing down from the Up-Pipe any more. Just trickling.

"Why did the Hoo-Mins send water down?" asked George. He was still trembling.

"Probably to Get us! Mama said they're the most dangerousest things in the world."

"Well, they missed us!" said George, sounding a bit more like himself.

"This time," said Harry. "But don't count your ants' eggs if we tangle with them again!"

14. Bright-Time Adventure

You might think that this adventure would have stopped George wanting to have anything to do with the dreaded Hoo-Mins.

But George had a short memory for fear.

"Those Hoo-Mins!" he said to Harry, only a few days later. "Trying to Get us with the water! How did they know we were there?"

"Don't talk about it," said Harry.

"They must be quite something!"

"Something to keep well away from."

"Yes. Sure. Except—"

"What?"

"I do just want to see one!"

"WE ARE NOT GOING UP THE UP-PIPE, and that's IT!" shouted Harry.

"I didn't mean that. I meant, we could sneak up a tunnel during the bright-time and have a peep at one."

This couldn't help seeming like a pretty exciting idea to Harry. He had a picture in his mind of a Hoo-Min. It looked like a tree that could move, with two feet like hairy biters.

He looked at George for a long time and waved his feelers about in a slow and thoughtful way. Suddenly they shot straight up. This is a centi's way of saying "YES! Let's go for it!"

George made lots of humps along his back with excitement.

When the next night ended, they were put to bed (as we would say – they didn't have beds like ours, of course; they crawled under damp leaves that Belinda had dragged down the tunnel). George was staying over in Harry's nest. Belinda tucked them in and kissed them. She did this by making sure their leaves were damp and passing her feelers gently over their heads.

"Good bright-time. Sleep till night-time. Mind the ants don't have a bite-time," she said, to tease them. (That's the nearest I can get to what she said in Centipedish.)

Then she went off to her own rest. Full-grown centipedes go to sleep at the same time as centis. So Harry and George didn't have long to wait.

As soon as all was still, they crept up an up-tunnel. Harry was trembling with excitement. Before long they could see bright light coming down. They were not used to light and they didn't feel comfortable. Centipedes can't close their eyes. So they tilted their heads downwards and felt their way forward with their feelers.

They hadn't reached the tunnel's entrance when they heard that thumping again! It was right overhead.

"It's a Hoo-Min!" crackled George. "Walking on its hairy biter feet!"

But now it was Harry who felt brave.

"Come on! Let's peep at it!"

They crawled the rest of the way up the tunnel towards the light.

15. Looking at a Hoo-Min

As soon as their two little heads poked out of the tunnel, they saw it!

Only they didn't recognise it at first. They were looking for a tree with cat-or-dog feet. And this was something quite different – as you know, because what they saw looked very like you. Only a lot bigger.

Their weak little eyes were almost dazzled by the bright sunlight. But standing just a little way away was a – well, what could they call it? A Thing. A monster. They had never seen or

dreamt of anything half as big, awful and scary.

"Is that one?"

"It must be!"

"It's not – it's not a bit like I thought!" crackled Harry.

"No!" George crackled back. "It's worse!"

The Hoo-Min came towards their tunnel. They shrank back into it.

The huge feet thumped the ground, which shook and trembled. The two centis cowered down. One foot slammed right down over the hole, shutting out the light. For a second there was darkness. Then the foot lifted and the light shone in again.

The thumping got fainter as the Hoo-Min walked away.

George and Harry cautiously lifted their heads above the ground and watched it go.

"It – it makes the mole-cricket look like an ant!"

"I bet even hairy biters and belly crawlers are scared of Hoo-Mins!"

Then George said something unbelievable.

"Let's follow it!"

Harry let out a great crackle. "ARE YOU CRAZY?"

"Its eyes must be in that round part at the top. How could it see us? It's so far up from us. Let's just run after it and see what it does!"

And without waiting for Harry, George scurried out of the tunnel and took off on all his forty-two legs, after the Hoo-Min.

16. Belinda to the Rescue

You've probably noticed that Harry nearly always did what George did.

But not this time.

After dithering for a bit, he turned and ran back down the tunnel to his home-nest. Belinda was there, of course, fast asleep.

"Mama! Wake up!" crackled Harry.

Belinda shot out from under her leaf.

"What? What is it? Is it a belly crawler?"

"No, Mama! It's a Hoo-Min!"

If centipedes could turn pale, Belinda

would have become a white centipede.

Her front feelers waved so wildly they bumped into each other and twisted together. It was like a person wringing their hands.

"Where?" she breathed at last.

"On – on the no-top-world, Mama."

Belinda untwisted her feelers and seized Harry with her pincers.

"What are you frightening me for? Where else would a Hoo-Min be? We're quite safe down here! Hx, if this is your idea of a joke—"

"But Mama – Grndd is up there too!"

Belinda let Harry go.

Grnddjl – Grndd for short – George – had no mother. It was his own fault for leaving her, but the fact was, he had no one to look after him. No one but Belinda.

She didn't waste time asking any more questions.

"Come on," she said, and began racing up the nearest up-tunnel.

Harry raced after her.

Halfway along it, she stopped dead and Harry ran into her rear segment.

Without a crackle, she turned round, ran back, ran along another tunnel, stopped, listened, and turned again.

All the time Harry was trying to follow her, bumping into her, having her run over him as she turned, and then running after her again. He couldn't make out what she was doing. But suddenly he heard the thumping overhead again, and he understood.

Belinda was trying to find out exactly where the Hoo-Min was, above them.

Now she ran into another tunnel.

Belinda knew the network of tunnels very well. She knew how to get to the surface in the right place – nearest to the Hoo-Min.

They poked their heads out of the tunnel. The brightness fell on them. It hurt their eyes. But they put up their feelers and scented the air with them.

Harry sensed the Hoo-Min at once. It had a very strong smell and it put out a lot of heat. Even in the hot sunshine he could feel it in his sensitive feeler-tips. The Hoo-Min was very close to them. So close its shadow fell on them.

"Can you sense Grndd?" Belinda asked.

They were both waving their feelers desperately in all directions.

"Yes! He's over there!" said Harry, pointing both feelers.

"I sense him. I'm going to fetch him."

"No, Mama! Don't! The Hoo-Min—"

"Stay here! Don't you dare come out till I get back!"

17. The Hoo-Min Strikes

Belinda dashed out of the hole.

She headed straight for George, who was hiding under a bit of stick. He'd followed the Hoo-Min for quite a long way and was now watching it, fascinated.

He didn't see what the Hoo-Min was doing. But Belinda did.

The Hoo-Min was bending and straightening. It was lifting things.

It was lifting *sticks*.

Its big feeler was reaching out. *It was reaching for the stick that George was hiding under.*

Belinda ran, signalling frantically for George to come to her, but George wasn't noticing anything except the Hoo-Min. It was so big and so close that George couldn't make out what it was doing – until the stick that was covering him was suddenly lifted away.

George was out in the open! The Hoo-Min could see him!

The Hoo-Min straightened up. Its shadow covered everything as it raised its top leg with the stick in its feeler.

The stick it had just picked up came down again. Very hard. *WHACK*! Right on the ground where George was. If centipedes could shriek, Belinda would have shrieked. But after all, the stick didn't land where George was, but where George *had been* half a second before.

He shot out of the way just as the stick
came down.

The stick came
down again.

And again.

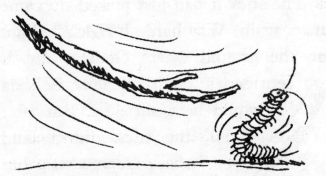

It beat the earth.

Whack! Whack! Whack!

George ran frantically here and there,

dodging the stick. But he couldn't really dodge it. He didn't know where it would hit next. He was more frightened than ever before in his life.

He just twisted and turned and raced here and there. It was only good luck that the beating stick kept missing him. Sooner or later, it must find him!

Suddenly the stick fell to the ground. The Hoo-Min let it go.

George stopped running.

He looked around. The Hoo-Min was leaving the ground and coming back to it very heavily. The noise and vibrations were thunderous. It kept making noises from its head, as well. Noises that sounded like "OW! OW! OW!"

Can you guess what had happened?

Right! That brave mother centipede, Belinda, had run up the Hoo-Min's trouser and given its leg a mighty bite!

18. The Run for Safety

The moment she'd done it, she ran down the leg again to the ground. She had to keep running, because the Hoo-Min was jumping up and down and its great feet might have landed on her and squashed her flat.

As soon as she was clear of the jumping, she turned and looked for George.

He was right beside her.

He'd seen her dashing away from the howling Hoo-Min, and had followed her.

"Grndd! Come with me, quickly!" Belinda signalled.

He didn't need to be told. As fast as she ran, he ran faster. I told you centipedes can run very, very fast. Well, even I didn't know they could run as fast as George and Belinda ran then.

They reached the hole where Harry was hiding and fell into it on top of him. The three of them rolled down the slope, all tangled up together, and lay at the bottom. They looked like a shiny lumpy black ball with about a million legs sticking out in all directions.

I'm exaggerating. But three times forty-two is quite a lot of legs. And two-thirds of them were awfully tired from running.

Harry was the first to uncurl himself and become a separate centipede again.

"Mama? Why did it start going up and down like that, and making that funny noise?"

"I bit it," said Belinda shortly.

Both the centis stiffened their front feelers in astonishment.

Then, as if they were one centi, they rushed up the tunnel again and poked their heads out.

The Hoo-Min was nearer the ground now, all hunched up, bent over its leg and making another kind of noise. Like "Ooooooogh, uuuuuuugh, aaaaaaaaah!"

They ran back to Belinda.

"You couldn't have bitten it! It's still moving!"

"Well, that's partly why they're so dangerous. Biting them doesn't kill them. It doesn't even paralyse them. They're too big."

"So why is it making that noise? Why did it stop trying to kill me?"

"I think because it hurts," said Belinda.

"Maybe if all three of us bit it—?"

"*No*, Grndd," said Belinda. "No. We will go back to our nest."

Neither George nor Harry felt like arguing.

Back in the nest-tunnel, both the centis felt very tired and wanted to go straight to sleep. But Belinda had something to say first.

"I don't know if you've learnt a lesson, Grndd," she said grimly.

"Oh yes," said George quickly.

"I doubt it. I don't think anything can teach you not to get into trouble. But I have to try. Bend over."

That's what she would have said, if she'd been your mother, perhaps. Centipedes can't bend over. What she

91

actually said was more like "Bottom up!"

Anyway, George knew only too well what she meant.

19. George Gets a Spanking

George, trembling with alarm, turned round and stuck his rear segment into the air.

Belinda stood beside it.

She raised her first foot on that side. She brought it down hard on George's back end.

The next little while wasn't much fun for George, because that was only the beginning.

Belinda walked past his raised rear segment and spanked him once with each foot. And as if that wasn't enough, she then turned round and walked past him the other way, spanking him once with each foot on her other side.

So that was twenty-one spanks on one side, and twenty-one more on the other. Forty-two spanks altogether. It seems a lot, but that was a normal punishment for a disobedient centi.

Mind you, it really doesn't hurt half as much to be spanked if you've got a thick cuticle on your bottom. So it wasn't as bad as all that.

When it was over, George lowered his tingling rear segment to the ground, and rubbed some of his nearest legs over it. If centis could sniffle, George would have sniffled.

"Now, centis, go to your leaves," said Belinda sternly.

There were no kisses for either of them.

George crept away under his leaf.

He felt very,
very sorry.

I can almost hear you saying it: "Sorry he'd been so bad? Sorry he'd put Belinda into danger?"

I'm afraid not.

What he was sorry about was that he'd had a spanking from Belinda. He forgot she'd saved him. He just thought how his bottom hurt and how she wasn't even his real mother.

Which was pretty ungrateful of him.

But if you'd just had forty-two spanks, you might not feel grateful either. Even if your life had just been saved.

And in case you're wondering if Belinda had managed to teach George not to get into trouble, don't even think it.

She hadn't.

Because I'm afraid George – and here comes a wonderfully useful word for people like him who won't learn to be sensible – George was *incorrigible*.

20. Smoke!

A few days later, when Harry was just about ready for sleep, his mother started chewing up his bedding and spitting the bits on the floor.

"Mama! What are you doing?"

"I've got a nice new leaf for you," she said, with her mouth full. "I'll just use this old one for floor-lining. Come and give me a mouth."

So Harry helped, and soon his old bed-leaf was well crunched and spat out and spread smoothly over the floor of their nest. The spitty part dried and Belinda rubbed her head over it until it had a sort of shine and it looked very nice, the way new floor-tiles or a carpet would to us.

"Good centi! Now, come and choose a new leaf to sleep under."

There were plenty of leaves to choose from. Belinda had worked hard, dragging them down the tunnel. They were all shapes and sizes, and quite soft, juicy and colourful, not crackly and dull like his old one.

"How come there are so many?"

"This is the season when some of the trees drop their leaves," she explained.

Harry chose a pretty yellow one which was just the right size for him and curled up under it and went to sleep.

In the middle of the day he was suddenly, and not at all pleasantly, woken by George landing on top of him and bashing him in the head with his own head.

"Get up! Get up! Something terrible's happening!" George crackled.

Belinda shot out from under her own new leaf, and so did Harry.

They didn't have to ask what the terrible thing was. They could immediately smell it and sense it and even see it, despite the darkness.

Even Belinda, who had lived the longest and seen all the seasons round, had never seen this before.

It was all around them, in their breathing holes, in their eyes, tickling their feelers. They were dreadfully frightened. Yes, Belinda, too. It was so strange, so uncomfortable, so – George hadn't exaggerated – so terrible!

It was smoke. But they didn't know that. They had no word for it, and no word for "mist" or "fog" or "cloud" – nothing to compare it with. Things are so much more frightening when you don't

have words for them... They just knew it
was something to run away from.

They left their cosy nest and ran.

21. Escape

They ran blindly, without thinking.

Lots of others were running, too – other centipedes, and hundreds of other underground creatures – ants and beetles and bugs, and bigger things too. Things the centis would normally hunt, or be hunted by. Now none of them were thinking about eating each other. They were just fleeing from the smoke that was drifting down the tunnels from the surface.

It was coming from a bonfire that a Hoo-Min had lit, to burn the leaves. But what do centipedes know about bonfires?

They only knew they were choking and terrified.

They ran. Their many swift legs carried them fast and far along the tunnels. They kept together. They ran instinctively along down-sloping tunnels because these were freer from smoke.

That was how they found themselves in the water-cave under the Up-Pipe.

There they stopped. They were too

tired to run any more. The smoke in their breathing holes made them weak. But down here there wasn't any smoke. At least, not yet.

"Maybe we'll be safe here," said Belinda.

Safe? Safe, under the Up-Pipe?

"Mama, we're not safe *here*!" said Harry. "The Hoo-Mins send water down the Up-Pipe to Get us! Last time we were here, we nearly—"

Belinda turned round slowly and looked at Harry.

"The last time you were *here*?" she said. "The *last* time you were here? How many times have you been here, since I told you NEVER NEVER NEVER to come here?"

"Two times," said Harry at last, hanging his little round head.

Belinda sank to the ground.

"You might as well have left when my other centis did," she said sadly. "You don't love me. You don't listen to me. You don't care what I say. I might as well not be your mother."

Harry threw himself on top of her.

"Mama! That's not true! Of course I love you, of course I care! It was just..."

But he couldn't think what it was "just". He couldn't remember now why he had disobeyed his mother.

George said bravely, "It was my fault. I talked him into it," but Belinda hardly heard him.

She just kept lying there, shaking her head sorrowfully and saying, "You came to this worst-place-in-the-world. You didn't believe me. I was trying to keep you safe."

Harry kept touching her gently with his front feelers, trying to tell her how sorry he was.

"Please, Mama," he said at last, "let's get out of here. It's dangerous, honestly! The white-choke stuff is safer than this! At least it doesn't drown you!"

But even as he crackled, some of the white-choke came creeping down the tunnels after them. It began to fill the water-cave.

(In case you're interested, the Hoo-Min on the surface had been pumping smoke down a hole to kill snakes and other things, and it was spreading right through the network of tunnels. But the centipedes didn't know that.)

Belinda jumped up on to her forty-two feet.

"We can't go back up that tunnel!" she said. "Let's run alongside the water-channel – maybe there are other tunnels at the other end!"

But even as she crackled, they felt that smoke was coming stealing towards them from the far darkness at the other end of the cave!

It was coming thicker and thicker, spreading itself all around them. It had even reached the bottom of the Up-Pipe and was beginning to creep upward!

22. The Living Ladder

George and Harry remembered at the same moment.

"The earth-pile! Quick!"

Belinda watched, puzzled, as the two centis began frantically pushing and shoving at the loose earth with their heads and front legs.

"What are you doing?" she cried. "We must run! We must—" But she had to stop because the smoke was getting thicker.

And suddenly she understood.

"NO!" she crackled as loudly as she could. "Not that! Not Up the Up-Pipe, I tell you, NO!"

But George and Harry took no notice. They had quite a high pile of earth now. It was nearly tall enough for George to reach the bottom rim of the Up-Pipe with his front four pairs of legs.

Not quite, though.

Now each time they shoved a bit of earth to the top of the pile, to make it higher, it rolled back down. They were not going to make it!

Suddenly Harry stopped digging and piling and looked at his mother.

"Mama," he said. "Come here. Come quickly."

Belinda wasn't stupid. She saw what Harry wanted. As the white-choke got thicker, it overcame all her other fears.

She ran up the side of the earth pile. She stood upright on the top. She easily reached the rim of the Up-Pipe.

She got a good grip on the inside of the pipe with her front eight pairs of legs.

"Climb!" she said.

Her segments were as good as a ladder. The two centis ran up her body faster than you could run upstairs.

They were inside the Up-Pipe.

Belinda's urgent signal crackled after them: "Keep going! Hide up there and come down when it's safe! Don't look back, I'm all right!"

23. Up the Up-Pipe

Once they were in the pipe, they just kept climbing.

The inside of the pipe was smooth and it was wet. Every now and then, they slipped. But their sharp little feet found places to grip on to and always they kept struggling upward.

Neither of them looked back. They just kept going.

Luckily the pipe was not very long. Quite soon they were at the top. They came up through a little hole. It was a drainage hole for a shower, but they didn't know that. The shower was in a shower-room, and the shower-room was in the home of a Hoo-Min. But they didn't know that, either.

The two centis scrambled out. They were not standing on earth. They were standing on something smooth and hard. They listened. Nothing! They crept further from the hole and began to explore.

They ran around two sides of the small room (not that they knew about rooms). Then they found a long opening – a crack – that they could run through. They were so muddled up and frightened and tired that it was only when they were about to run through this crack that Harry thought to look around for Belinda.

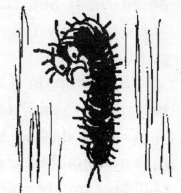

She wasn't there.

He rushed back to the hole and looked down. It was dark down there. A trickle of white-choke came up. He couldn't see anything.

"Mama!" he crackled.

From the door-crack George signalled, "Come on!"

"I can't! I can't leave her!"

"If she wanted to come up, she could, easily."

"But why would she stay down there? – MAMA!"

"She told us to keep going, that she'd be all right! She knows all the tunnels. She's probably found another tunnel to go home by!"

"She wouldn't leave us. I'm going back down!" said Harry.

George dashed back to the drainage hole and grabbed Harry by a back leg.

"You are not going back down there!" he said. "She helped us get up here, that's what she wanted! She wants you to obey her. Do what you're told, for once! Come on, we must find another way to get out before a Hoo-Min comes!"

Very unwillingly, Harry took his head out of the hole and let George pull him to the door. They didn't know it was a door, of course. They went under the bottom of it and found themselves in an enormous black-dark place. It wasn't no-top, but the top was so far away that at first they thought they must be outside. But there was no earth under their feet and it all smelt strange and horrible.

It smelt of Hoo-Min, and Hoo-Min food, and shut-in-ness, and it scared them silly. It also mixed them up.

They ran for a long time, alongside a straight-up-hard-thing. They were trying to find a hole or any way out, but they couldn't find one.

They were getting very, very tired.

The hard cold stuff began to hurt their feet. But that wasn't the worst.

It was warm in that place. And dry. And into the hearts of the two centis came a great fear. Not just that they would never escape. But that they would Dry Out.

"I think – I think we should go back down the Up-Pipe," said Harry.

"If we can find it," said George.

Harry stopped running.

"It's over that way," he said.

"No, it's not. It's over that way." George waved his feelers in the opposite direction.

They looked at each other.

"Hx," said George slowly. "I think we're lost."

24. Bad Smell and Silence

They huddled together in a corner of the room.

"I hate this awful place!" said George.

"It stinks so badly I can't smell where there's water," said Harry.

"Listen," said George. "Do you hear anything?"

They both listened. It was very silent. In the earth tunnels there are always little noises, but not here. It was very spooky, not being able to hear or see, or sense anything familiar.

"What shall we do?"

"I don't know."

"I wish Mama was here!"

"So do I!"

But she wasn't. So they had to think of something to do by themselves.

"Let's – let's get away from this straight-up-hard-thing," said George.

They turned inward and started cautiously toward the middle of the room.

They felt terribly scared. While they'd been next to the straight-up-hard-thing, at least they had felt protected on one side. Now they could be Got-at from all around. The silence and the unknown

smells added to the awful
scariness.

They kept bumping into
each other, not by accident.
Just to feel that the other one
was there.

At last George whispered,
"There's something just
ahead." He couldn't see
anything but his feelers knew
it.

They found it. It was hard
and cold. It, too, went straight
up but it wasn't a wall.

It was shaped like the
water-post. They could walk all
around it.

"It's like – it's like the

outside of the Up-Pipe," said Harry, which was a very clever thing for him to say, because what it actually was, was a hollow metal bed-leg.

"Let's climb it," said George. "Maybe there's water up there." He was beginning to feel very dry.

It was hard to climb but no harder than the Up-Pipe. Quite soon they found themselves climbing something much easier. It was soft and loose, like lots of spiders' webs put together, only not sticky. They scrambled up it and found themselves on a flat surface. It was made of the same soft, warm stuff.

They almost liked it. It was kinder to their feet. They ran about on it and would even have played, if they hadn't still been so scared, and they hadn't been feeling so dry. Besides, the smell was suddenly much stronger.

Harry ran up a hill and down the

other side. The hill was even warmer. George followed. They kept running and exploring in the dark.

"Hx! Here's a tunnel!" crackled George excitedly.

25. The Blanket Tunnel

They ran into a deep, warm tunnel. It was nothing like earth; it was made of the warm-web stuff.

Still, it felt wonderful after the openness of the floor. They felt covered and safe. They ran along, one behind the other, George first. Harry, behind him, ran faster, and ran right over George so he could be in the lead.

But the smell was very, very strong in here.

Harry stopped suddenly. George bumped into him.

"What?"

"There's something strange here."

George came alongside and they felt the strange thing with their feelers.

"Well, it's meat, that's for sure," said George.

Suddenly the two centis realised that the smell they'd been smelling was a foody smell. But it was something they'd certainly never eaten.

"I'm hungry," said Harry.

"Me too," said George.

"Shall we– ?"

But they didn't. Something stopped them from having a bite. They kept feeling the meaty thing, which blocked the tunnel. It rose steeply in front of them – a meat-cliff. They felt and felt. George felt in one direction, Harry in the other. After a while they ran back to each other.

"This meat-cliff is only part of it, whatever it is," said Harry.

"It's huge," said George.

"It goes on and on," said Harry.

"No end to it," said George.

"It's got bumps and hollows," said Harry.

"Some parts are hairy," said George. "It must be some kind of hairy biter."

"Maybe," said Harry. But the most ghastly thought had come into his head. He dared not say it.

They were quiet for a moment. Then George said, "Let's climb up it!"

Harry said slowly, "You know what I think it is?"

But George didn't want to listen. "We can't stay here!" he said. He began scrambling up this big warm meat-mountain.

Harry couldn't bear to be left behind. He scrambled up after him.

26. The Meat Mountain

They climbed up a straight place that had wrinkles on it which made it easy to climb. It was the sole of a foot, but they didn't know that.

When they got to the top, they slipped between two knobbly things. These were toes. But they didn't know that.

They ran down a gentle slope, dodging between stiff hairs, and came to a long thing like a branch, except that it was hairy too. Here, the roof of the warm tunnel lay right on top of them and they had to push through. But they were used to burrowing, and this was easier than that.

At the other end of the branch – which was a long way – they came to a smoother part. It was like a big flat warm meaty floor. No hairs here.

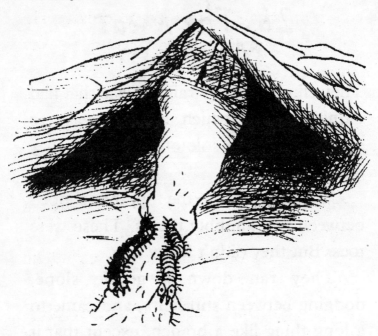

"Stop a minute," said Harry.
"What?" panted George.
"Why is it going up and down?"
"I don't know!"
"I do," said Harry. "It's breathing."

That stopped George, but only for a moment.

"Let's go on!"

"Grndd," said Harry.

"Oh, what?" said George crossly. He sensed that Harry was going to say something he didn't want to hear.

"I think – I think – we may be climbing on a Hoo-Min," said Harry quietly.

At these dreadful words, they both crouched down in terror. But after a while, George stood up again.

"Well, it's not doing us any harm," he said. "Maybe it's dead."

"I sometimes think you're stupid," said Harry. "It's not dead. It's warm and it's breathing. If you ask me, it's asleep."

That made George brave again.

"Listen," he said. "What's the most important thing for us right now?"

"To get home," said Harry.

"No," said George. "That's second-most-important."

"To get damp," said Harry.

"Right," said George. "And I smell water."

Harry moved his feelers around. He could smell it too, now. It was rather a long way off, but he knew it was ahead of them, not behind.

Harry knew they were doing the thing Belinda had warned him never to do. He was sure they were in terrible danger. But when a centipede feels itself drying out, nothing else seems to matter except getting damp.

"All right," he said at last. "Let's head for it. When we're damp, we'll be able to think better."

They began to run across the flat meaty floor towards the moist smell.

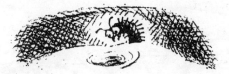

27. The Lovely Wet Tunnel

They passed a nice little nest on their way – just the right size for one of them to curl up in. (It was a tummy button of course, but they didn't know that.)

They were both very tired by now. George got into the little round nest and turned around in it several times. When he curled up tight, it just fitted him.

"You can't rest now, Grndd!" crackled Harry. "We must go—"

Suddenly there was an upheaval. Something came down hard on top of the warm-web above the little round nest. Huge hard things moved around,

prodding and scratching, and the whole vast meat-mountain they were on heaved and shook.

George shot out of the nest just in time. The two centis clung together. Then, as the prodding things went on digging and rubbing at the little round nest, they scattered and ran.

They ran on through a heaving forest of hairs. This was tricky for them. The hairs grew so thickly here that they had to push through. Several times their little claw feet got caught on the hairs and they had to pull free.

The hairy forest moved up and down even more than the hairless floor, even after the whole meat-mountain had stopped heaving about. And then The Noise started.

It was a rumbling, gurgling, growly sound, a little like thunder, but wetter. It happened – then stopped – then it happened again. It kept on happening.

"What's that noise?" asked Harry fearfully.

But George didn't even bother to answer. His cuticle was feeling drier and drier. His breathing holes were all dry around the edges. His feelers, back and front, were so dry he felt they might snap off if he bumped them.

He could sense the water. It was getting nearer! Nothing else mattered. He made for it, and Harry, though quaking with fear, followed.

At last they came out of the forest and found a meaty ridge in front of them. There was no warm-web tunnel roof over their heads now. They were in the open.

They ran along the ridge. There was a great curly complicated bit of meat at the top. They found a tiny tunnel in the middle, and stood for a moment, peering in. Should they go down it?

But the moist smell was not coming from there. It was close by, though. They ran over a prickly slope, and suddenly, there it was – a round hole, rather like the top of the Up-Pipe only it was made of warm meat.

They stopped on the edge and peeped in. The noise was coming from here and it was very loud, but they just didn't care.

"A lovely wet tunnel!" breathed Harry.

"Oh, Hx! We made it!" said George.

"LET'S GO!" they both cried together.

And they threw themselves down into it.

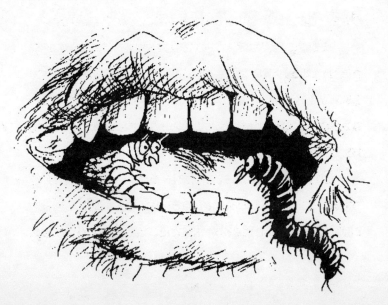

For about two beautiful seconds, they ran around the inside of the tunnel, getting themselves gloriously damp again.

Two seconds was all they had.

After that, everything started to happen.

28. The Earthquake

In the country where the centipedes lived, there were sometimes earthquakes. Not very big ones. But the centis knew about them, knew what happened when the earth shook and tunnel roofs fell in and you had to dig yourself out.

What happened when they were in the wet tunnel was worse than the worst earthquake they had been through, or could imagine.

First of all the tunnel suddenly seemed to jump – a very big jump, not a little jump. The two centis clung on to a big wet thing inside their tunnel with

their
forty-two (well,
eighty-four counting both of
them) feet, but not for long, because
suddenly they were flying through the air.

Not just flying nicely like a bird on the breeze, but like a cork flying out of a bottle. Like a bullet fired from gun. Well. Not quite that fast, but it felt that fast to them.

Of course you can guess what had happened. They had popped down into the sleeping Hoo-Min's *mouth*. And he had felt them running around, and it had wakened him, and he had leapt up and spat them out as hard as he could. PTUI!

Of course, you and I can think of

nothing
much worse
than   having a
couple of centipedes
crawling around
inside our mouths. The poor
old Hoo-Min, you might think!
No wonder he spat them out and
sent them flying through the air.

But think of poor Harry and George!
They had forty-two feet apiece but they
didn't have wings. Flying through the air
was about the worst feeling they'd ever
had. Even worse than nearly drowning.
But it didn't last as long.

A moment, that's all. Then they
landed back on the bed.

Luckily it was soft. They weren't hurt, just frightened out of their wits.

They ran around in circles for a minute or two. And then suddenly it was bright-time.

Light flooded them. They crouched down. Then a shadow fell on them.

They both knew what they had to do when a shadow fell on them.

Run. Run! *Run*!

29. The Chase

They ran.

They ran across the warm-web thing. But it wasn't good for running on! Their feet kept falling into the open bits of the blanket and snagging in the tiny hairs of the wool.

They kept expecting something to whack down on them. But the Hoo-Min was looking for something to hit them with. That gave them a few moments, long enough to reach the edge of the bed.

They headed straight down. Luckily they found the bed-leg and slid down it head-first.

Then they were on the floor. They ran across it like mad, heading for the door. They could see it now.

The Hoo-Min had found something to hit them with. It was a rolled-up newspaper, but they didn't know that. All they knew was that something came down – CRASH! – just behind them as they ran.

They shot forward, faster than ever.

The Hoo-Min could see them quite plainly. He saw the way they were running. There was nothing wrong with his eyes, or his aim. Yet he kept missing them.

The reason was, he just couldn't believe how fast they were running. He aimed at where he thought they would be, but by the time the newspaper landed, they were always a little bit further on.

They reached the door of the shower-room. The newspaper came down

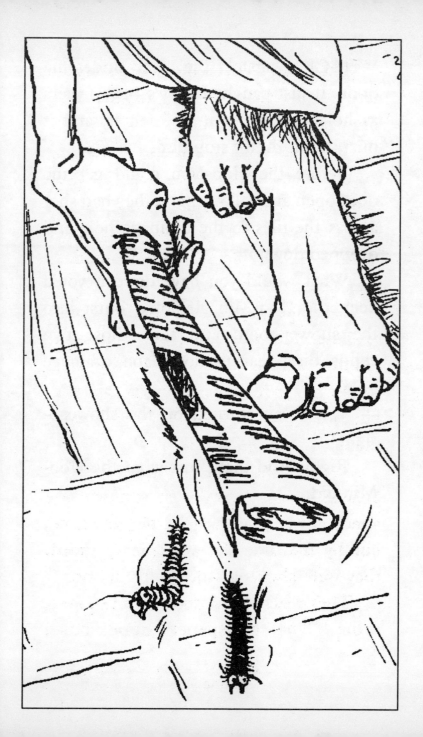

WHACK! against the crack under the door. It just caught Harry's back feelers as he raced under it. He felt it, and it hurt, but it didn't stop him.

Before the Hoo-Min could get the door open and follow them, they had shot across the tiles to the drainage hole and dropped down it.

What would you have done if you'd been the Hoo-Min? If you'd burst into the shower-room and seen those two centis disappearing down the drainage hole?

You'd have turned on the shower – right?

Right. And that's just what the Hoo-Min did.

30. Down the Up-Pipe

Harry and George had had some good luck and they'd had some bad luck on their adventures. Now they had the best bit of luck they'd had so far.

They just didn't know it.

What happened when the Hoo-Min turned the tap on full was that – *nothing happened.* Not a thing. Where this Hoo-Min lived, things didn't always work properly. And sometimes there was no water for a while.

By a wonderful piece of good luck (for the centis) no water came out of the shower to wash them away and maybe drown them. Not a single drop.

So they shot down the Up-Pipe and fell on the earth-pile together in a tangle, and no jet of water shot down after them. A lot of noise did follow them. It was the Hoo-Min saying bad words in a very loud voice, but the centis didn't know that.

They untangled themselves and stood up. Most of the white-choke was gone and they felt terrific. Triumphant! They'd done it! They'd actually climbed on a Hoo-Min and survived! They felt like a pair of the bravest centis who ever lived!

"Wait till we tell Mama!" crackled Harry. "Wait till—"

And then they saw her.

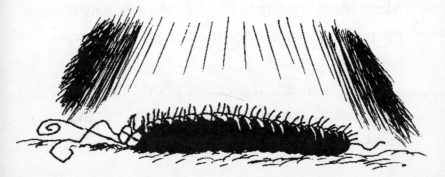

She was lying at the bottom of the earth-pile. They saw her in the light coming down the Up-Pipe.

She was lying in a crumpled heap. She looked like – she looked like – she looked like – a very dead centipede.

31. The Long Way Home

"Mama!"

They ran their front feelers all over her body, and Harry tried to make her wake up by pushing her head with his.

"Is she dead?" asked George in a whispering crackle.

"No! No! She can't be! Mama! Wake up, wake up!"

But Belinda didn't move.

"We've got to get her home!"

"How can we? She's so big!"

"She's no heavier than the mole-cricket! Come on!"

George didn't say anything more.

But what he was thinking was that the mole-cricket was *much* smaller than Belinda, and that when they brought home the mole-cricket, it was almost all downhill. The long way back to the nest was nearly all uphill.

But they had to try.

They got hold of Belinda's front feet and dragged her, and when they couldn't drag her any more they tried getting behind and pushing her, but that didn't work, so they had a rest and then

dragged her some more.

It was by far the hardest thing either of them had ever done, and it just went on and on. When they thought of the length of tunnel still to come, they both wanted to lie down and give up.

What kept them going?

Harry kept going because Belinda was his mother. George kept going because Harry did.

They both kept going because they knew they shouldn't have put themselves first, and left Belinda at the bottom of the Up-Pipe in the white-choke.

They both kept going because they could imagine how they would feel, for the rest of their lives, if they didn't.

But the worst thing they each thought of, though neither of them said it, was that perhaps it was for nothing.

Perhaps she was dead all the time.

At last, just as they thought they were going to have to give up, something wonderful happened.

As the centis were dragging Belinda along, they felt her get a little lighter. They looked along the length of her body and saw that her back legs were moving. A bit of her was walking, helping.

"Mama! You're alive! You're alive!"

Belinda's head moved. They felt her front feet moving too.

"Try to walk, Mama! Help us get you home!"

And she did. Slowly at first, and then, as more and more of her legs started to work again, she moved by herself.

The centis danced at her side, encouraging her. It wasn't that much further anyway – they'd nearly got her back all by themselves.

Soon they came out of the tunnel into the nest.

Belinda fell to the ground and the centis pulled her leaf over her. She stopped moving and her feelers drooped, but they knew she was just asleep this time.

The air in the nest-tunnel was almost clear again. The white-choke was gone, though they could still smell it a little, enough to remind them how awful it had been.

Harry and George crept about, being quiet.

"Aren't you hungry?"

"Starving! What I couldn't do to a lizard right now!"

There were no lizards, but luckily Belinda had caught a couple of beautiful fat spiders, four ants and a grasshopper the night before. The two hungry centis ate the lot, sharing the grasshopper between them.

Although they were tired, they decided to go hunting for something for Belinda to eat when she woke up.

They went to the no-top-world.

32. The Toad Hunt

It was a lovely quiet night – the moon shone down through the trees and made dappled patterns on the leafy ground – just the kind centipedes feel safe in. Harry and George ran around and played in the moonlight.

"Wasn't it awful, though? – the Hoo-Min!"

"We actually climbed on it!"

"Don't tell your mama, she'd kill us!"

"She was right about them. They are the scariest things in the world. But I must tell her! She'll be so proud of us!"

"Don't count on it! I'd keep quiet,
if I were you," said George, rubbing
his bottom with his back legs
rememberingly.

After a while they got hungry again,
and that reminded them what they'd
come out for.

They spotted a young toad squatting
near a patch of wet ground where the
Hoo-Min had been watering its
garden.

They raced each other up to the toad.

It tried to hop away, but they caught
it, overpowered it with their poison-
claws, and were soon dragging it back to
their tunnel.

By the time Harry and George got
home, Belinda was better. She'd got up
and was waiting for them.

"My wonderful centis!" she said, and
gave them a centi-kiss with her feelers.
"Thank you for helping me home! And
now, I want to hear everything."

Harry's wish to tell his mother

everything had gone. He didn't know quite how she'd take it. So he said, "Er – well, we spotted this toad, and—"

"No, No! When you went Up the Up-Pipe!"

"Oh, that."

"Of course I know you were both lucky and didn't meet a Hoo-Min, or you wouldn't have come back alive."

"*You* did, Mama," said Harry.

"*I* did?" asked Belinda, puzzled.

"When you went up. When you were young."

Belinda crouched down and they saw her feelers quiver. "That was very different. Your father was with me."

Harry stiffened with astonishment.

"My *father*?" He hadn't known he had a father. He'd never heard about him.

"I meant to tell you when you were older," said Belinda. "I didn't want to make you sad."

She looked so sad herself that Harry was afraid to hear, but he had to. "Tell me now, Mama!"

33. A New Word

"Your father was a brave centipede. When we went Up the Up-Pipe together, we were young and foolish, and we didn't know what was up there. The Hoo-Min chased us, and your father—" She stopped.

"Yes? Go on!" crackled Harry.

"Your father turned on the Hoo-Min and attacked him, and let me escape down the Up-Pipe. I... I never – saw him again." She dropped her head and trailed

her front feelers on the ground, a sign of
deep sorrow.

Both centis were speechless.
"He gave his life for me, so I could
look after you and the other little centis in

my basket," Belinda said quietly. "It's time you knew, Hxzltl."

"So that's why you told me never to go Up the Up-Pipe," Harry breathed. "That's why it's the worst place in the world for you."

"I never dreamt," said Belinda, "that one night I'd send you up there myself, and that it would save all our lives."

They were all very quiet. The toad lay among them and nobody thought of eating it. George was thinking, "Maybe the Hoo-Min we climbed on is the very one that killed Hx's daddy." The idea made his cuticle cold on his back.

That was when Harry said, in a choky crackle, "My daddy was a hero."

Only he didn't say "hero". There was no word, then, for hero in Centipedish.

He made one up, and afterwards it spread
– the way new words can – until all
centipedes now use it to mean "the
bravest of the brave".

What Harry said was, "My daddy
was a centipede-who-tackled-a-Hoo-
Min."

And in case you're wondering if, in
that case, Harry and George became
centi-heroes, because they'd actually
climbed on a sleeping Hoo-Min and gone
into its mouth – they didn't.

They didn't because they never told
Belinda, and they never told any other
centipedes about their adventure. They
kept quiet because they knew they
hadn't been brave – only reckless and
foolish.

But every once in a while, when
they were alone together, they would
nudge each other, and one of them would
say...

"I wish we'd had just one good bite each, though – don't you?"